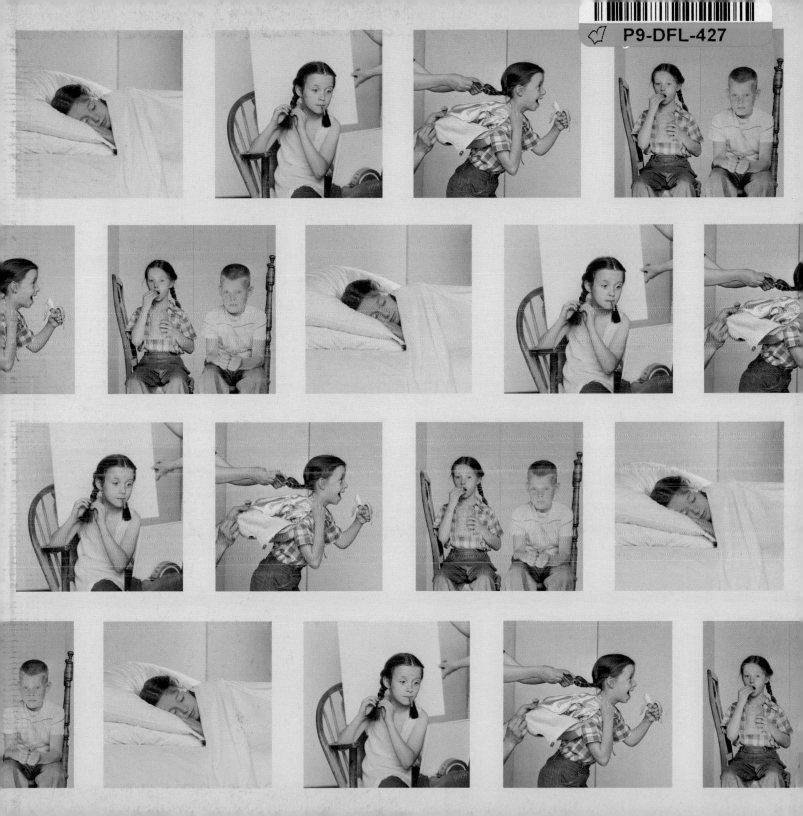

# Norman Rockwell's
# A Day in the
# Life of a Girl

**Norman Rockwell Museum**

The Norman Rockwell Museum houses the world's largest and most significant collection of Rockwell art. The Museum presents, preserves and studies the art of illustration and is a world resource for reflection, involvement and discovery inspired by Norman Rockwell and the power of visual images to shape and reflect society. The Museum advances social good through the civic values of learning, respect and inclusion and is committed to upholding the rights and dignity of all people through the universal messages of humanity and kindness portrayed by Norman Rockwell.

Norman Rockwell Museum, 9 Glendale Road/Route 183, Stockbridge, MA 01262  nrm.org

**Resources**

For more information about Norman Rockwell's life and work, excellent background can be obtained from the Norman Rockwell Museum website and Norman Rockwell's autobiography (currently out-of-print), *My Adventures as an Illustrator*.

**Writer/editor:** Will Lach
**Production manager:** Louise Kurtz
**Designer:** Ada Rodriguez

First published in 2017 by Abbeville Press, 116 West 23rd Street, New York, NY 10011

First edition
10 9 8 7 6 5 4 3 2 1

ISBN 978-0-7892-1290-0

Library of Congress Cataloging-in-Publication Data is available upon request.

For bulk and premium sales and for text adoption procedures, write to Customer Service Manager, Abbeville Press, 116 West 23rd Street, New York, NY  10011, or call 1-800-Artbook.

Visit Abbeville Kids online at www.abbeville.com.

# Norman Rockwell's
# A Day in the
# Life of a Girl

Written by Will Lach

Abbeville Kids

A DIVISION OF ABBEVILLE PRESS

New York · London

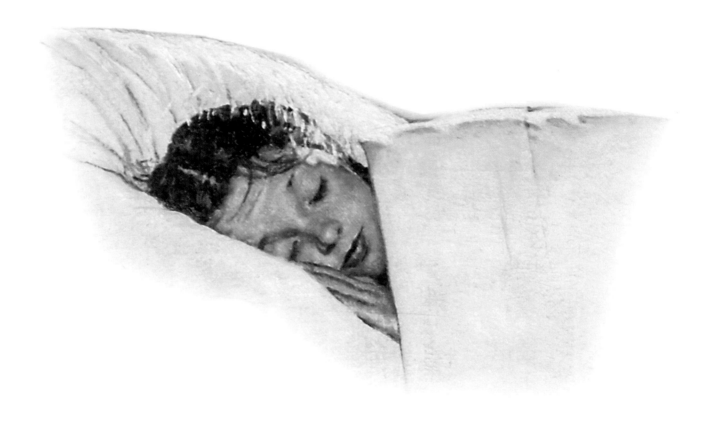

In the morning, my bed's
the world's quietest place,

But it's time to wake up,
yawn, stretch out my face.

I open my eyes
and tidy my braid,

Grab my swimsuit
and gobble
the breakfast I made.

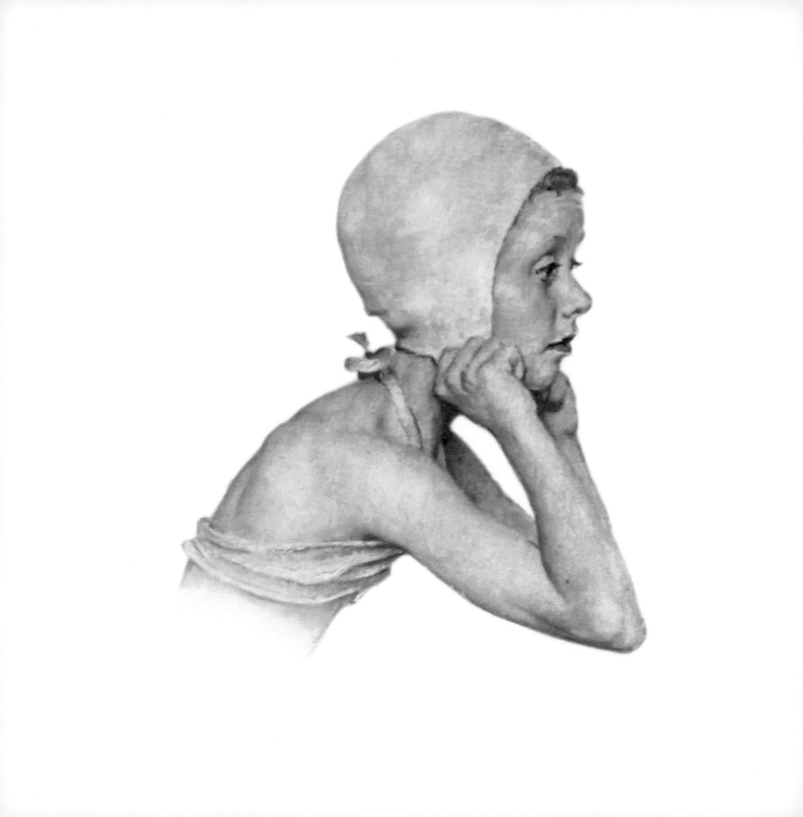

At the pool I slip into
my suit and my cap,

Jump into the water,
with a big backward slap!

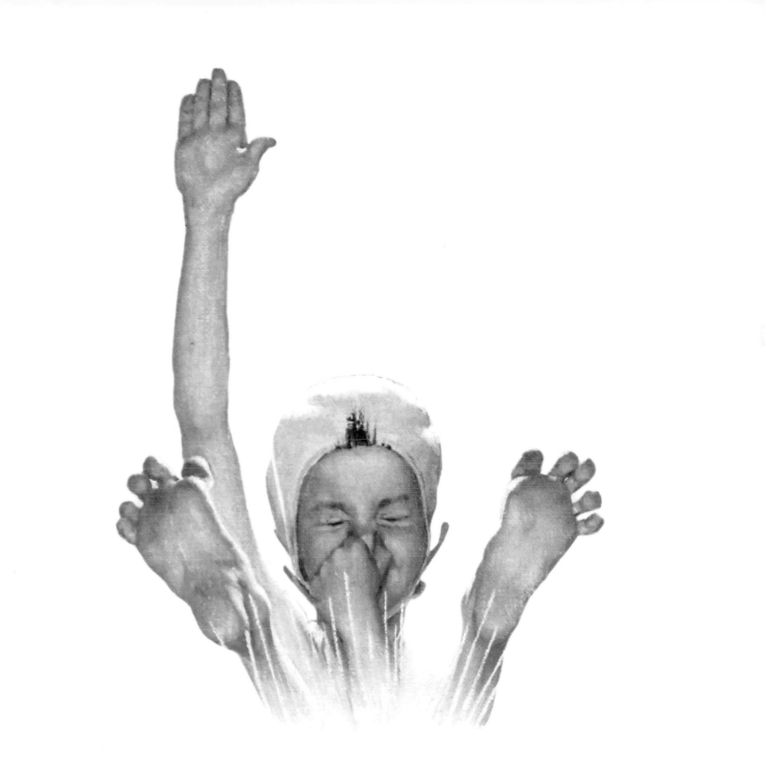

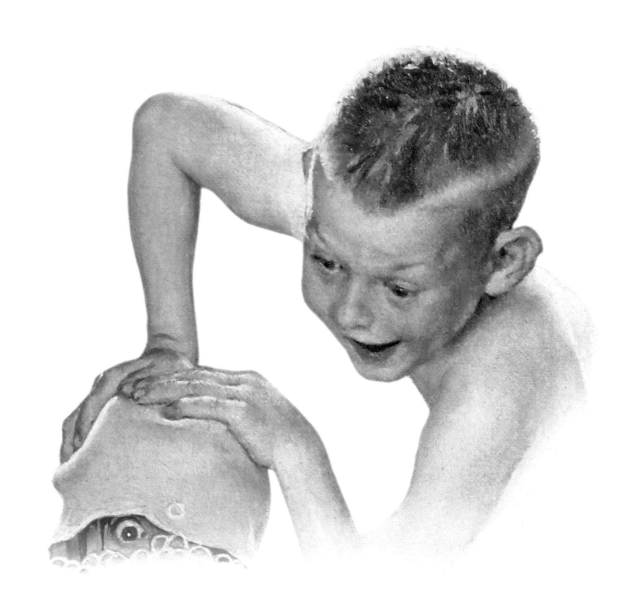

But then Chucky—that brat!—
comes and pushes me under,

He laughs, but I yell,
"You just made a big blunder!"

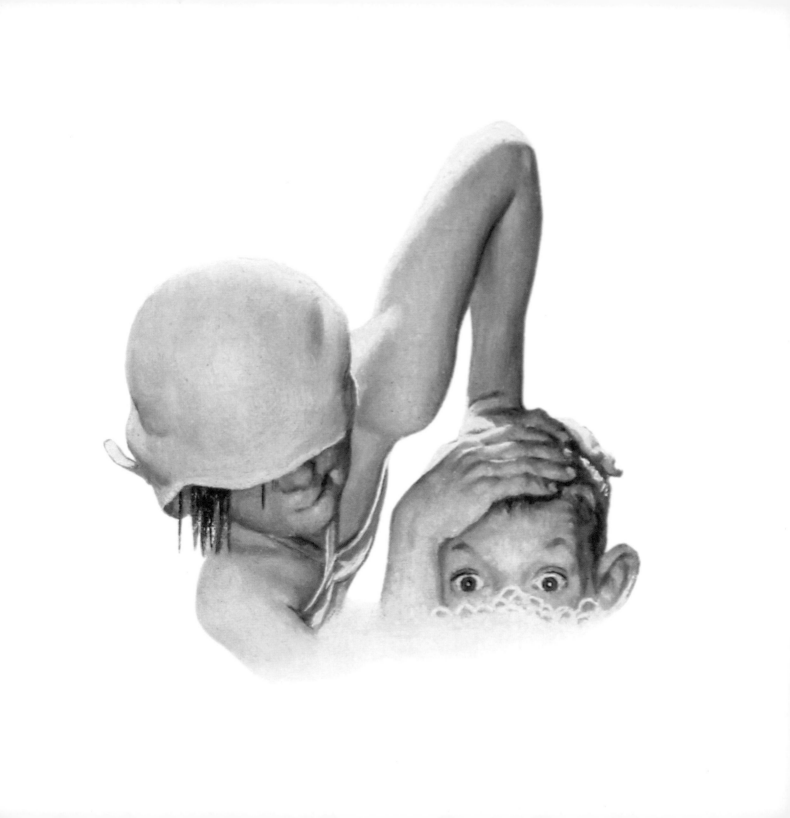

I spring up from the bottom and dunk him, all right.

But he comes back
with "I'm sorry"
and offers a bite.

We get dressed and go out
for a ride on his bike,

To the matinee show
of a movie we like.

We've both seen it before,
but we love a good fright.

Then it's time to go home—
there's a party tonight!

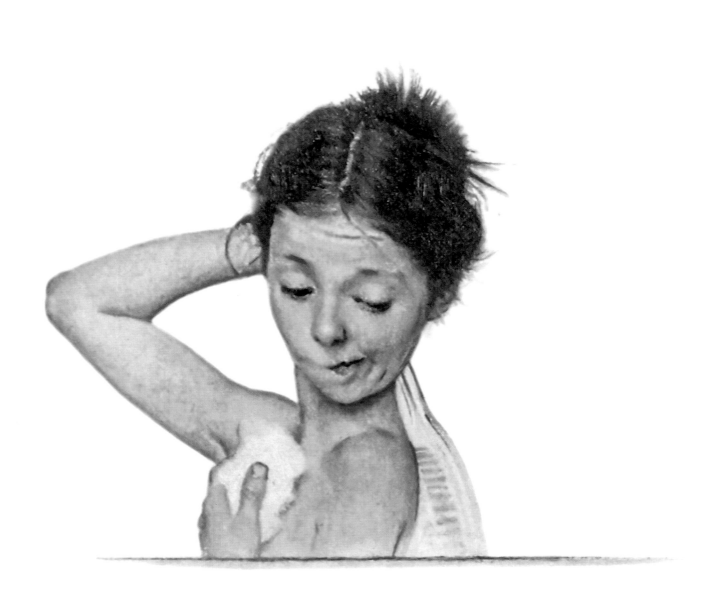

I scrub in the tub
for almost an hour—

My mom's shampoo smells like the prettiest flower.

At the party, there's fun,

lots of noise, chocolate cake....

When it ends,
there are candy-filled
baskets to take.

A peck on the head's
not a pleasant surprise,

But I write it all down,
with so-sleepy eyes.

I lock up my diary
and then say my prayers.

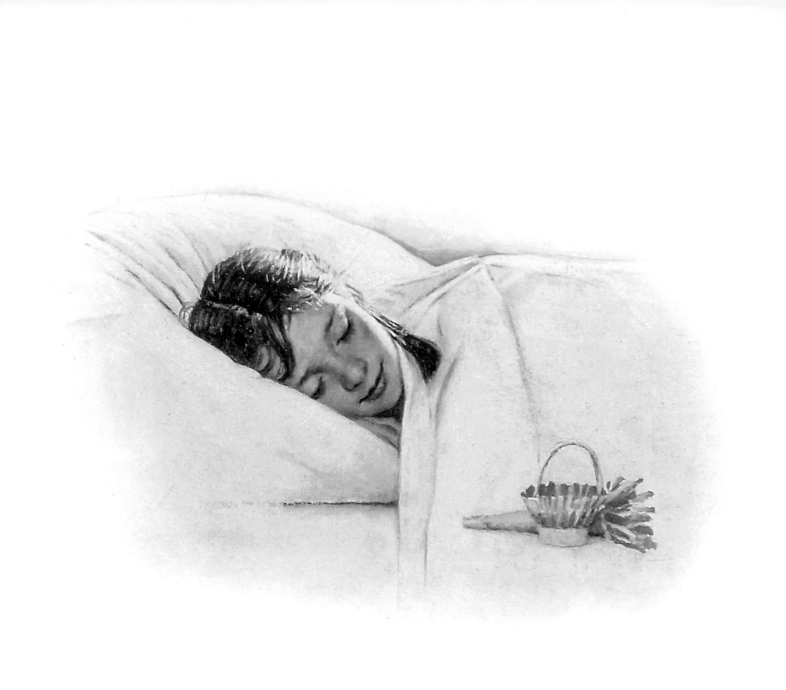

Ah, the end of a day—
and a night—without cares!

# About Norman Rockwell

NORMAN ROCKWELL was born on February 3, 1894, in a "shabby brownstone" in New York City.

Young Norman always wanted to be an artist. As he put it, "My ability was just something I had, like a bag of lemon drops. [My older brother] Jarvis could jump over three orange crates; Jack Outwater had an uncle who had seen a pirate; George Dugan could wiggle his ears; I could draw."

By age 14, Rockwell enrolled in art classes. He put everything into his work and, two years later, was paid to illustrate four Christmas cards. While still a teenager, he began to illustrate magazine covers, work that he pursued for nearly the rest of his life.

Rockwell's family didn't have a lot of money, but they spent every summer in the country, staying at farms. "We helped with the milking, fished, swam in the river, … trapped birds, cats, turtles, snakes, and one glorious morning a muskrat." Rockwell said that those summers "had a lot to do with what I painted later on."

In 1921, Rockwell moved out of the city for good and, eventually, settled in New England country towns: Arlington, Vermont, and Stockbridge, Massachusetts. He married Mary Barstow, a schoolteacher, and the couple had three sons, Jarvis, Thomas, and Peter. His work began to reflect small-town American life, and he often used his family and neighbors as models.

Toward the end of his life, Rockwell painted pictures of some of his deepest interests, including civil rights, America's war on poverty, and the exploration of space. In 1977, he received America's highest civilian honor, the Presidential Medal of Freedom. On November 8, 1978, at age 84, he died in Stockbridge.

# The Real-Life Girl of *A Day in the Life of a Girl*

*One of Norman Rockwell's favorite models was* **Mary Whalen Leonard**. *Mary posed for several of Rockwell's most popular works, including* A Day in the Life of a Girl. *This is her story.*

I grew up in Arlington, Vermont. I have a family of my own now—my husband and I have a son, two daughters, and six grandchildren—but I was nine years old when Norman painted this picture.

Arlington's a little village. As a girl, I was a tomboy, and I had three brothers, so I was out all the time, playing all kinds of games. The boy in the picture is Chuck Marsh. He and my brother were best friends, so Chuck and I grew up together. We skied together, and in high school I was his girlfriend.

I just loved going to the studio and working with Norman. It was a wonderful experience of being with somebody who loved what he was doing. Norman would say to me, "You and I are going to do *this* together this morning." And then he'd show me a little sketch, and he'd say, "Do you think you can do it?" And then we went right to work.

When we were posing for *A Day in the Life of a Girl*, there was a real party for the party scene. The cake was demolished, as it is in the picture.

**The Saturday Evening POST**

August 30, 1952 - 15¢

CALIFORNIA'S WEIRD OVERFLOWING SEA
By Keith Monroe

Helen Hayes Tries Hollywood Again
By Pete Martin

The little guy eating the ice cream was really a hellion. He was so much fun, but we had to move quickly to get this picture done because he was ready for cake and ice cream!

When we finished posing, Norman had a little bell that he rang. It was like magic—all of a sudden, the woman who worked for him would come out with a Coke for each of us. In those days, a Coke was the most wonderful thing in the world!

When the magazine came out, I would come home from school, and my mother would greet me, and say, "The *Post* cover came out today," and I would just take a glance at it, and put it down—I didn't really know what it was all about.

I was probably about 18 years old before I sat down and said, "Oh, yeah. I *did* this." And I think that was the gift in my life. I was just living my life, and this was part of it.

**Left:** Norman Rockwell, Mary Whalen Leonard, and Chuck Marsh outside Rockwell's studio in Arlington, Vermont, ca. 1952.

**Above:** "A Day in the Life of a Girl," *The Saturday Evening Post* cover, August 30, 1952. The images in this book were taken from the original oil on canvas painting made by Norman Rockwell, from which the *Post* cover was made.